Praise for Cindy Procter-King

"Cindy Procter-King is a master storyteller. Not only do her characters invite the readers into the drama, the humor is non-stop. Comedy is a hard genre to write but Cindy Procter-King does it easily."

— The Road to Romance on HEAD OVER HEELS

"What a set-up for a comedy of errors! Everything that can go wrong in this scenario does go wrong, and the reader is well entertained by the comedic chaos."

— Fallen Angel Reviews on HEAD OVER HEELS

"I really enjoyed *Borrowing Alex*. It was smart and funny without being overdone. The characters do some pretty funny things in the name of love. I am definitely looking forward to reading the next book I find by Cindy Procter-King."

—Joyfully Reviewed on BORROWING ALEX

"I really like romantic comedy as a genre, but it takes some really good writing to make me laugh. This book made me laugh."

— Fallen Angel Reviews on BORROWING ALEX

"'*Getting Over Brett*' is everything a romantic comedy should be!...a very funny, light and easy romance that will leave a big goofy smile on your face!"

— InD'tale Magazine on GETTING OVER BRETT

"*Getting Over Brett* is a top-of-the-line read. It has everything you could possibly want in a modern romance. It's fun and playful at times, full of flirty banter, then deeply romantic and emotional at its heart. Somehow, it's both sweet and sexy all at the same time!"

— Julianne MacLean, USA Today Bestselling Author

"Cindy Procter-King presents readers with a suspenseful snapshot of a romantic comedy... loaded with humor, this is a must-read."

— Night Owl Reviews on PICTURE IMPERFECT

"Procter-King has written a 'home' for all of us. Destiny Falls is the place that holds your first love, your first triumph..."

— RT Book Reviews on WHERE SHE BELONGS

Catching Claire

Also by Cindy Procter-King

Steamy RomCom

Love & Other Calamities

RomCom Series

Deceiving Derek (Book 1)

Before Brady (Book 3)

Just Janie (Book 4)

Trusting Trey (Book 5)

Love in the Pacific Northwest

Stand-alone Romantic Comedy

Head Over Heels (Book 1)

Borrowing Alex (Book 2)

Getting Over Brett (Book 3)

Contemporary Romance

Catching Claire

CINDY PROCTER-KING

Blue Orchard Books

CATCHING CLAIRE

Copyright © 2023 Cindy Procter-King
Second edition, expanded and revised

First edition © 2012 Cindy Procter-King

All rights reserved.

No part of this publication maybe be reproduced in any form or by any electronic or mechanical means, including information storage and retrieval systems, or otherwise, without explicit written permission from the author, except in the case of brief quotations used in book reviews and articles.

This is a work of fiction. Characters, names, places, events, incidents, scenarios, opinions, brands, media, are of the author's imagination or are used fictitiously. Any resemblance to actual incidents, locales, or persons, living or dead, is entirely coincidental.

Published by Blue Orchard Books

Cover by The Killion Group

ISBN: 978-0-9880884-5-0 (eBook)

ISBN: 978-1-989113-06-6 (Print)

For my mom, who always goes after what she wants

Chapter One

Just after midnight, Saturday, July 15th
Countdown to Tania and Trey's wedding: 14 days
(unless...)

STRIPPING off his clothes in a room packed with rowdy women was not Ridge Pederson's idea of a good time. But how could he refuse when the gigs paid a nice portion of his medical school bills?

Ridge exited the elevator, patting the coins in the pocket of the PJ pants riding low on his hips. As he strode toward the apartment building's laundry, the sour scent of alcohol lifted from his clothesbasket. His nose wrinkled. Over the last month, raucous bachelorette parties had crammed his summer weekends. Women pawed him, stumbled against his naked chest, 'forgot' to tip him. Or the big winner—they puked on his lap.

Thankfully, no one had upchucked during tonight's job, although the future bride had offered him a sip from her sticky cup, sprinkling his cop costume.

Ridge shouldered into the laundry room, balancing the hamper beneath an arm. Several feet away, a curvy brunette wriggled her bounteous booty in front of the bulletin board. Ridge peered at her. Claire Merriweather? The polite beauty who'd hired him for tonight's festivities danced in a short purple nightie that did wonders for her shapely thighs. As she bopped on spiky sandals, she tucked a messy wave of chocolate-brown hair behind one ear. Two dangling cords likely attached to a phone tucked...somewhere interesting, he'd bet.

She must own one super-tiny phone.

The sight of Claire dancing without a care in the world almost made up for tonight's annoyances. Almost.

Because her singing sucked.

The heavy door slammed shut as Ridge walked past her jiggling butt. He placed his hamper on the first washing machine. Throughout his performance in a fourth-floor apartment of this same building, Claire had arranged snacks and mixed drinks in the tiny kitchen. Then, she'd worn a simple white blouse tucked into jeans. Her courteous voicemail reserving his services in no way matched this animated dancing. Purple panties peeked from the hem of her floaty top. She swung a plastic cup and belted questionable lyrics.

"I copped a feel and then kissed it! Oh, yeah. Oh, yeah," Claire sang in a peel-the-paint-off-the-walls soprano. "The tip of his—la, la—nightstick!" Her cup rocked. The creamy concoction splashed onto the floor beside a humming dryer.

"Hello," Ridge called.

Her eyelids flitted half-open. She patted an earbud and continued her mangled version of karaoke.

"Hello!" Ridge strode toward her, thumping the washers.

Her gaze riveted to the bulletin board.

He cursed. Any loser might waltz in and see her. Take advantage of her. Maybe attack her.

Claire licked a flyer pinned to the cork. *Licked* it!

He stood behind her as she tongued the ad a second time. *His* ad. For his stripping business.

In the flyer, he wore the cop costume she'd requested for the party. Stainless-steel handcuffs dangled from his thick black belt, and he gripped a strategically positioned nightstick.

Singing, Claire Merriweather tore off every tab. She stuffed the papers into the frilly material at her cleavage.

Ridge narrowed his gaze. His second summer of med school was in full swing, and he'd worked his ass off to achieve his dream of becoming a doctor. *Nobody* messed with his tuition money.

Voice harsh, he tapped her shoulder. "Excuse me?"

Claire shrieked and jumped. Her drink flew out of the cup, splashing the flyer. One earbud popped free, and the cord swung around her bare shoulders.

"Sorry!" Ridge's hands shot up. What was he thinking, touching a customer, startling her? "I hit the washers to catch your attention—"

A loopy grin split Claire Merriweather's face. "It's you! My cop-a-feel!" She plopped the cup onto the droning dryer and flung her arms around his neck. Her lush breasts crushed his T-shirt, and a sweet whiff of Irish Cream liqueur drifted from her lips.

Ridge pushed her an arm's-length away and

held her there. Not that he didn't appreciate her enthusiasm. In fact, a part of his anatomy appreciated it *too* much.

"You were at the bachelorette party tonight," he reminded her, in case her neurons had misfired. "You hired me for your friend, Tania. I danced with her in Alicia Maxwell's apartment. Remember?"

Claire lifted a shoulder. "I wouldn't say I hired you for Tania."

Ridge flicked his gaze over her cute-as-hell attire. The tabs with his phone number fluttered from inside her top. Her purple nightwear—baby dolls, that was it—featured wide shoulder straps. Slippery fabric nipped at her waist and flared at her hips. He liked the tiny white bows dotting the hem. He liked the large bow centered on her cleavage even more.

That said, up close, on a spicy scale of one to ten, Claire's loungewear rated a three. The neckline didn't plunge, and the skirt covered her ass—when she wasn't bouncing around. The papers poking out of her top and the dangling cord gave her the appearance of a sexy, disorganized burglar on a midnight heist.

"Yes," he stated. "You hired me to dance for Tania Hoyt. She's the bride." He hadn't gyrated his hips for the wrong woman throughout his performance, had he? Impossible. Someone would have complained.

"I 'member," Claire slurred, and her beguiling dimples flashed. "Hey. Do ya twit?" She giggled. "How about video posts? You'd get a ton more calls."

Ridge's grip on her upper arms slackened. His social media game was bang-on, but that wasn't the point. "If you hadn't destroyed my *ad*, I'd get all the bookings I need."

Her gaze lowered to his plaid flannels, which he wore commando.

She looked back up, her pale green irises shining. "You pack quite a package, Ridge."

He rolled his eyes. *May lightning strike me dead. Now. I'll donate my body to science.*

Two weeks ago, when Claire hired him, her voice on the phone had sounded practical. Sensible. They'd discussed his rates and his arrival time at Alicia Maxwell's apartment, the duration and heat level of his performance. He had no problem flirting with partygoers or stripping down to a leather G-string. Unlike some event dancers, he drew the line at simulating sex with the guest of honor. In tonight's case, Claire's friend, Tania.

"You're steadier on your feet now," he said, releasing Claire's shoulders.

Her hands slipped beneath his T-shirt. *Jeez!* Her palms skated over his abs and pecs. His flannels risked tenting in an energetic salute.

"*Do me,*" she whispered.

"Stop." Clutching her wrists, Ridge flipped her hands back out. "Claire, I don't know what you think I'm advertising"—other than the party dances—"but I will not sleep with you." Or any other client.

Her lips pursed, and his dick twitched. God help him.

"Not even if I leave a generous tip?"

"*What?*" Was she for real? "*No.*"

She pouted. "What's wrong with me?"

"Nothing. I don't pick up drunk women." Between the med-school grind and grabbing whatever work fit his busy schedule, he hadn't gotten laid in longer than he cared to consider. And she'd needed to remind him?

"I'm. Not. Drunk." Her bleary gaze indicated otherwise.

He released her wrists. "It doesn't matter."

She wobbled on her sandals. "You won't take me home?" She stomped a heel. "No one ever takes me home! No one says I'm beautiful. Everybody thinks I'm fat. No one loves me. Everyone loves Tania. Everyone loves Lacey. Alicia's dog worships *her*. But I'm unlovable!"

"You're not unlovable. And you're not fat." Not every guy wanted to date a human pogo stick.

Claire jutted a hip. "Would we have sex if I were five-seven and had great boobs?"

Ridge trained his gaze on her face. "You do have great boobs." From what he'd noticed moments ago.

"You're not looking at them. You're not feeling them." She launched herself forward. "Catch!"

"Careful!" He pushed out his hands—and her generous rack filled his palms.

Her loopy grin returned. "There. Now tell me they aren't great."

"I never said they weren't great." Ridge's throat tightened. Claire's breasts spilled over his fingers. Firm yet soft. Perfection.

Don't look down.

He looked down.

His thumbs nudged the center bow on her top. His fingers pressed the papers against the ivory skin above her modest neckline.

Look back up, Pederson. Don't squeeze these babies. Not even once.

Claire slumped against his chest, and her temple banged his chin.

He squinted. "Claire?" But her mouth had relaxed with sleep, her eyes sealed shut.

He groaned. She'd passed out with her hot knockers stuffing his hands.

What the hell did he do now?

Chapter Two

Coffee. She smelled coffee. And something fruity. With milk.

Claire's stomach roiled. *Gross. Not milk.* Not when her brain cells were on the verge of curdling.

The bright mid-July sunshine streaming through Alicia's living room window pierced Claire's closed eyelids. Moaning, she buried her pounding head inside the sleeping bag on the sofabed. The chilly zipper bumped her nose, but the soft pillow cradled her aching skull. A few gratifying seconds of silence passed. Then an annoying munching sound assailed her ears. Was someone eating cereal?

Claire's nostrils flared. Alicia usually kept an assortment of tasty cupcakes from her shop or healthy muffins on hand.

The munching grew louder. Claire's temples throbbed. *Please stop with the munching. Oh, please stop. Ohhh, pleeease. S-T-O-P. Stop.*

Her mouth tasted like the heel of a sweaty sock. And she only had herself to blame. She rarely drank. Yet how many Mudslides had she consumed last night? Four? Five?

Vodka, Kahlua, Baileys, and way too much light cream had topped her glass. The drinks had tasted amazing then. Now, the memory churned her insides.

She huddled in the sleeping bag as fuzzy memories blipped in her brain. Last night, Alicia hosted a combination bridal shower and bachelorette party for Tania's closest friends. In this apartment. Where Claire had planned to sleep overnight.

As maid of honor for Tania's wedding occurring in two weeks, Claire had felt obligated to take part in her best friend's merrymaking. Sadly, neither of them possessed a high tolerance for alcohol. Throughout the party, Tania had jabbered about the sexy stripper Claire had hired as a surprise. The women were drooling by the time the guy left. Especially Claire.

During his performance, she'd huddled in the kitchen, declaring herself the official bartender so she wouldn't over-ogle his deliciousness. Afterward, fearing her lust would reflect in her eyes, she hadn't met his gaze while paying him.

Yes, everything was coming back to her in murky snatches.

The cereal-munching continued. She eked out a raspy whisper. "Stop."

The TV snapped on. Sports news blared, but the chewing mercifully quit.

A lull. Blissful.

Claire breathed in the sleeping bag's cozy campfire scent. Her brain cells snapped to life, and her eyes popped open. She stared at the orange lining of the bag.

Oh, no. Alicia had promised fresh sheets. And Claire's friend did not watch sports.

Footsteps neared the sofabed. The weight of someone far heavier than Alicia sat on the end of the thin mattress. Springs creaked.

Goosebumps speckled Claire's arms. "Alicia?" she mumbled into the bag.

The cereal munching resumed.

Claire held her breath and peeked out of the bag. A familiar naked male back blocked her view of the TV.

Oh, my God. The stripper from last night!

She gawked at his impressive shoulder muscles and thick brown hair two shades lighter than her own. A remote control sat beside his flannel-clad hip.

Why was he at Alicia's? Had he returned to the party after Claire passed out—uh, fell asleep? Had this super-hot dude and Alicia shaken the bedframe in Alicia's bedroom?

The stripper shifted on the mattress and spooned more cereal into his mouth. His broad shoulders tapered to a trim waist above loose red plaid PJ pants—

Crap! How did Claire know his bottoms featured a relaxed fit? Fortunately, they did, because last night his flesh version of a nightstick had packed his G-string to mind-blowing proportions. Claire would die of embarrassment if he turned his head and caught her eyeing his crotch.

Which happened in the next second.

"Good morning, Claire," the stripper said. His lips crooked in a sexy smile, and he muted the TV. "Feeling okay?"

"Uhhh." Her mouth dropped open as a memory of his PJ pants and a droning dryer flashed through her mind. Forget Alicia! Had *Claire* and this supremely built stripper done the bouncy in the apartment building's laundry on a freaking dryer?

"Who are you?" she blurted.

His smile widened. "Ridge."

"No." She inched her fingers out of the sleeping bag. "Not your stage name. Your real name."

"That is my real name. Ridge Pederson." He shoved another spoonful of colorful cereal into his mouth and chewed. The fruity aroma wafted above the sofabed.

"Ridge?" she parroted, brain foggy. She glanced around the apartment. Cappuccino-colored walls swam into her field of vision. Alicia's walls were beige. And where were the party streamers? The balloons?

She blinked at the marigold-yellow sofa arm. Where was Alicia's blue-and-white-striped couch?

"Where am I?" The answer stared her in the face. She was in *his* apartment. In his bed. Her ancient MP3 player rested on a side table, along with a set of tangled earbuds. Tiny papers printed with his phone number and stripping-specific socials littered the dark wood. *"We slept together?"* she croaked.

He chuckled. "You don't remember?"

She sat up against the couch and shoved the

sleeping bag to her waist. The air cooled the baby dolls another friend, Lacey, gave her before the party's scavenger hunt. Claire loved the gift, a thank-you present for helping Lacey land a pitch for her lingerie designs with Claire's employer, a Seattle investment group.

Her belly cramped. She raked her fingers through her hair. When had she changed into Lacey's creation? And why?

"Of course I remember," she wheezed.

"I don't think so," Ridge responded.

"What does that mean?"

He held the cereal bowl in his left hand. "Number one, I'm good in the sack. You'd be more enthusiastic if you remembered. Number two, I wouldn't rock your world in a sleeping bag unless we were outdoors. Number three, this mattress murders my back. We'd have done it in bed."

Cocky much? "We *didn't* sleep together then. What a relief."

His eyebrows arched.

Her nostrils twitched from the fruity cereal smell. "How old are you?"

"Twenty-four. How old are you?"

"Old enough to know better." He was three years her junior. Claire prided herself on her maturity and self-control. She was pretty sure she'd called upon both characteristics last night. All right, sixty percent sure. Whatever. At least she hadn't thrown herself at a cradle-aged stripper named Ridge.

She massaged her thumping forehead. Another memory emerged. He hadn't *wanted* to sleep with her. The jerk.

"You have a problem with my name and age," he said around a mouthful of cereal. "Funny, you weren't this prim and proper in the laundry room."

Her face burned.

"Yep." He grinned. "That's where I found you. I liked the way you tongued my ad."

She glanced at the tear-off tabs on the table. Last night, the papers had hung from his photo.

"I did not," she protested. Except she had, judging from the pulpy taste lingering between her lips.

"From what I gathered," he said, "you stayed at Alicia's while she took her dog and drove Tania home."

More humiliating memories surfaced. Claire groaned. He was right. After her closest friends had needed to go, the remaining partygoers went clubbing, leaving Claire as the sole member of the cleanup crew.

Making the most of her time alone, she'd tried

on the baby dolls. She'd paraded in front of Alicia's bedroom mirror, admiring herself in the lacy nightwear one minute and obsessing over her physical imperfections during the next.

Hadn't fantasies of Ridge's steamy dance moves inspired her to bust a few of her own?

Lovely.

To top it off, she'd decided it was the height of efficiency to throw a load of Alicia's washing into the dryer—in the building's basement laundry, where Claire and Alicia had first spotted Ridge's flyer.

"This *is* Alicia's building, right?" she asked to double-check. "You live here too?"

"Yes, to the first question. No, to the second. I'm apartment-sitting. You were unsteady in the laundry. I took you to Alicia's, but she wasn't home. Neither was her friend across the hall."

"Lacey," Claire supplied.

Ridge nodded and scraped his spoon into his breakfast bowl. "From what you said, you left your phone inside Alicia's and couldn't remember her number."

Claire flinched. Damn booze. "Her door automatically locks. Didn't I take the key?"

"You're asking me?" His mouth curved in

another engaging grin. "You wouldn't tell me your street address. In case I was a considerate home invader, I guess."

"I'm sorry. I was tipsy."

"Uh-huh. You needed to sleep it off, so I brought you here."

Heart pounding, Claire glanced away as the worst memory from last night made itself known. She had *begged* Ridge for a hookup. If he wasn't a gentleman, he would've seen her jelly belly! And touched her thighs.

She dragged in a breath. "I need coffee." Gallons of it. "And toothpaste."

His brown eyes twinkled. "Coffee is in the kitchen. Also got orange juice."

Claire crawled out of the sleeping bag. She adjusted the top of her baby dolls to cover the bottoms before shuffling barefoot to the counter. A sugar bowl sat beside the coffeemaker, but no creamer. Not an issue. The thought of adding her usual dollop of dairy soured her stomach.

"I'll start with orange juice." She opened the fridge.

"Claire, wait!"

Too late. Her gaze fell on a plate on the middle rack. A mouse—its dead eyes staring and its tiny body misshapen, as if it had contorted itself into a parody of a contemporary dance routine—lay in a sealed bag between a block of cheese and a jug of orange juice.

Claire gagged. "Omigod! That is just sick."

Chapter Three

RIDGE PLUNKED his breakfast bowl onto the floor and ran into the kitchen. Damn it, he should have remembered Fargone's weekly meal thawing in the refrigerator. The sight of Claire's bouncing butt had knocked him into Stupid Land.

The fridge door slammed shut. Claire turned, face white. She dragged in air. "Why is there a mouse in your fridge?"

Ridge scrounged in the drawers for a paper bag. "Here. Breathe into this for a few seconds." He helped her position the bag around her nose and mouth, allowing space for a fresh flow of oxygen. Her lingerie-covered breasts grazed his naked chest. His skin tightened. "Six or seven deep breaths should do it. I'll count with you. One...two...three..."

Eyes wide, Claire followed his instructions. The paper bag inflated and deflated.

"That mouse must have been a shock," Ridge said, stepping back as she continued deep breathing. "Don't worry. The rodent is for the snake."

She squealed into the sack.

He lifted a hand. "The snake belongs to my dad. He's in the other room. Sorry, my *dad* isn't in the other room. The snake is. He's a three-year-old ball python named Fargone." Ridge counted her inhalations. Six slow, steady breaths. Her color returned. "Feel better?"

She nodded.

"Good." First, he'd freaked her out in the laundry. Now this. *Real smooth, Pederson.* "You can breathe normally. I'll take the bag."

Forehead crinkling, Claire handed him the crumpled sack. "You have a snake?"

Ridge empathized with her confusion. Hangovers were a bitch.

"Fargone is my dad's snake," he repeated. "This is my dad's apartment." He jostled a thumb toward the fridge. "Fargone's next meal is tonight. The mouse is thawing."

Claire shuddered. "You kill mice to feed your snake?"

He gave up on the ownership issue. "Feeder mice are dead when you buy them. It's no different from picking up a package of chicken thighs or ground beef for your supper."

"I'm turning vegan."

A smile tugged his lips. Claire had a sense of humor. He liked that.

He placed the bag on the counter and retrieved two coffee mugs.

"Fargone eats once a week," he said. "You just happened to come along the night before his next meal."

She squinted. "What kind of name is Fargone?"

"What sort of name is Merriweather?"

She glanced away. "I see your point."

Ridge poured a mug of coffee and handed it to her. "Want milk?"

"Black is fine." She sipped. "Oh, this hits the spot." She sipped again. "Thank you, Ridge."

"You're welcome." He poured himself a mug and added sugar. "My father is a herpetologist," he explained. "A reptile scientist. Fargone was a rescue snake. His previous owner was a meth addict. At one point, Far lost an eye. A neighbor took the snake to a shelter after the meth guy overdosed. The shelter workers were concerned. In another day, the poor snake would have been too 'far gone' to save. The name stuck."

The hint of a smile quirked on Claire's lips. "Didn't the neighbor know Fargone's real name?"

"The neighbor and the meth dude weren't close." Ridge gazed into her eyes. They were an unusual shade of pale jade green. "When it became clear no one wanted to adopt a one-eyed snake, the shelter contacted my dad for advice. His solution was to bring Fargone home."

She nodded. "Where is your dad now?"

"In China, exploring the Great Wall and visiting a Giant Panda reserve. It's his honeymoon. He and my new stepmom Ruth return in ten days. That's when I'll move back to my place near the university." Rosevale—the Seattle suburb where his dad, Alicia Maxwell, and Claire's other friend, Lacey, lived in the same building—sat too far from med school.

Claire's hands curled around her coffee mug. "Do you enjoy living in the U District?"

"Yeah. I have a couple of roommates. It's cramped, but it works." Ridge sipped his steaming java.

"I'm in North Seattle area too. Ballard. But I work downtown."

Ridge cocked his head. "Ah, the lady remembers something."

A blush stained her face.

Damn it, he'd screwed up. "Don't feel embarrassed, Claire."

"How can I not? I literally threw myself at you last night. If you weren't a gentleman—"

"But I am." Leaving his mug in the kitchen, he strolled to the sofabed and retrieved the red plaid robe matching his PJ pants. Both were last year birthday gifts from Ruth. He returned to Claire. "Put on this," he suggested, gaze drifting to the bow between her breasts. "Not that I don't like what you're wearing, but this robe is better. For both of us."

She blinked. "Is that a compliment?"

He grinned. "Yep."

She set down her coffee. As she slipped on the robe and wrapped the flannel around her lush curves, she asked, "Do you really have a one-eyed snake?"

"Counting Fargone?" Ridge allowed himself a half-smile. "I have two."

Her blush deepened. "Sorry. I meant your dad's snake. I have a horrible headache." She pressed three fingertips to her temple.

"I'll find aspirin."

Ridge went into the bathroom. He returned with the tablets and a glass of water. Claire stood barefoot, sipping coffee and studying the framed photographs on the living room wall. Most featured his dad and Ruth on their many adventures. In the last few years, they'd visited Israel, Peru, and now China.

"Here you go." Dodging his upturned cereal bowl, Ridge accepted her mug and passed her the water and pills.

"Thanks." She swallowed the aspirin and drained the water. She gave the glass back to Ridge. "I recognize these ruins." She took her coffee mug again and pointed at a photo. "What is this place called? The name is on the tip of my tongue, but... hangover." She combed a hand through her tangled hair.

Smiling, Ridge set the water glass on a side table. He walked closer to his guest. "Machu Picchu. It's in Peru." He showed her another photo of the ruins. "This is my dad and Ruth at the view from the Machu Picchu guardhouse. The small mountain in the distance is called Huayna Picchu. They climbed it later that morning. Dad asked Ruth to marry him on Huayna Picchu."

Claire's small smile flipped his arousal switch. Man, he'd love to wake up to a smile like hers. Kiss her until she moaned. Carry her to bed and explore her beautiful body until she called out his name. Over and over.

"Traveling is on my someday list," she murmured, voice husky.

He filed away the fantasy of morning loving and focused on their shared interests. "Same here. I need to finish med school first."

"You're a doctor?" Her wavy hair grazed the robe.

"I'm on my way. Stripping helps pay my bills. That and my other job right now." Plus his savings.

"What else do you do?"

"I shouldn't say. You might puke."

Claire laughed, her twinkling gaze reeling him in. "I like you, Ridge."

"And I like you. A lot." His last girlfriend, a fellow medical student, had seldom let loose. At first, he'd thought she was laser-focused on her studies. Nothing wrong with that. As time passed, he'd realized she wasn't a people person. She risked becoming a doctor with a poor bedside manner. That wasn't how he wanted to approach his career or his life.

"Tell me about your job," Claire said, nudging him. "I can handle it."

"I dissect cadavers."

Her eyes widened. "You do what?"

"Cut up dead people. For summer-session anatomy classes. The students don't dissect. They examine the samples I prepare."

She waved a hand. "That's enough. I mean, I'm interested. Just not now."

"You don't want to hear about the guy I worked on last week? He had this—"

She shook her head. "Triple sure."

"Too bad. It's fascinating."

"Another time." Moving to a cluster of photographs, she sipped the last of her coffee. "Is this your mom?" She gestured at a picture of a ten-year-old Ridge squinting into the sun with his dark-haired mother on a beach.

"Yeah. She lives in LA. She took off when I was two."

Claire's gaze softened. "I'm sorry."

"It's okay. We reconnected when I was eight." Ridge scrubbed a hand over his mouth. "When I was little, my mom had big dreams. She wanted to act."

"Oh? What was she in?" Genuine interest threaded Claire's tone.

"A few commercials. A TV movie. Now, she mainly teaches dance. She's fun to hang out with, but in some ways I feel closer to Ruth."

"Aw." Claire nudged him again. "I'm glad you got to know your mom. She sounds cool."

"She is. You asked about my name. Mom got it from her favorite soap opera. I can't remember the title of the show."

Claire gave a tiny shrug. "Look at the bright side. She could have named you Brick. He was a character in my mom's soap."

Ridge chuckled. "You surprise me, Claire Merriweather. You're serious but fun. And hot."

She glanced away. "About that toothpaste...?" She set down her mug.

He'd scared her off. "Meet Fargone first."

She fidgeted with the robe sleeve. "I'll pass. No offense. Alicia and I have a dress fitting at a Belltown bridal salon at noon. I should text her. She must be wondering where I went last night."

"She knows. You wrote a note on that cupcake-themed chalkboard hanging on her apartment door. You said you left with me and would return at eleven AM."

Claire smacked a palm against her forehead. "I don't remember that at all."

"You thanked her for dragging you to the laundry a couple of weeks ago. Otherwise, you might have missed my ad. You also wrote not to disturb us."

"This is getting worse and worse! I had to become a wordsmith last night?"

He turned up a hand. "Blame the alcohol."

"I will. Did I write your apartment number on the chalkboard? Your phone number?"

"Nope, and nope. I tried to scribble my info in a corner, but the chalk was tiny in my hands, and you erased the message." *With* the hem of his T-shirt. While he'd been wearing it. He'd squashed himself against the door so she wouldn't rip his clothes during her robust wiping.

"You were becoming rambunctious," he said. "I brought you here before someone complained to the complex manager. I tucked you straight into bed." He'd offered her the bedroom, but to Claire a conventional bed with a comfortable mattress and cool sheets meant having sex. Last night the idea had anyway. Twice after Ridge had dozed off, she'd snuck into the bedroom, and he'd walked her back to the pullout couch.

"We didn't fool around?" she asked, shaking her head. "We didn't kiss? Not once?"

He held up three fingers. "Scout's honor." Unless he counted her slobbering on his earlobe at four in the morning. He'd turned his head to avoid her lips.

She groaned. "Alicia must be tearing out her hair with worry."

"She seems nice. I'm sure she'll understand."

"She's not a fan of stupidity. What I did was dense."

"Enjoy the morning with me then." Ridge glanced at the news ticker along the bottom of the TV screen. "It's nine-fifteen. There's plenty of time to meet Fargone before you go." He didn't want this appealing woman to leave at all. His free Saturday nights were rare. He yearned to spend time with Claire. Talk to her, get to know her. Convince her that hanging around with a dancer named Ridge wasn't a bad idea. That it could be a *great* idea.

She chewed her bottom lip. "All right. First the toothpaste. Then the snake." She wagged a finger. "No feeding him in front of me. That's an order."

Ridge chuckled. "Yes, ma'am."

Chapter Four

CLAIRE STOOD at the bathroom sink, gaping at the horror show that was her reflection. Her hair looked like a flock of chickens had run amuck on her head. Dark smudges circled her eyes, and a zit protruded on her chin. Ridge hadn't mentioned any of this!

She pushed up both robe sleeves and opened the vanity drawer. Ruth's drawer, according to Ridge. The space contained an unused toothbrush. Claire glimpsed sealed mascara samples and unopened concealer. *Thank you, Ruth.*

Somehow, over the next ten days, before Ridge's father and stepmom returned, Claire would replace every borrowed item. She had no choice but to dig into the samples. She wasn't leaving this bathroom resembling a half-melted wicked witch.

Minutes later, satisfied with her repairs, she fluffed out her loose brown waves. Tania's mom kept hounding her to get highlights for the wedding. Should she? Ridge was smart, funny, generous, and undeniably hot. Plus, he seemed interested. He'd already seen her at her worst. Only a fool would walk away from the sparks simmering between them.

The thumping in her forehead receded to a dull ache. She untied the robe and plumped up the girls inside her top. She knotted the robe to expose the bow between her breasts.

Claire gazed at her reflection with approval. Okay, so today wasn't a true morning-after with Ridge. Not in the way she'd intended during her laundry escapades. But she looked pretty good, if she said so herself. Strike that. Her curves looked amazing. A hint of cleavage winked above the purple silk, and she smiled into the mirror. She didn't need no damn highlights.

"Go get him, tiger," she whispered at her reflection.

Drawing in a deep breath—Real Life Claire wasn't as brave as Mirror Image Claire—she returned to the living room. Ridge wrung out a dish-cloth at the kitchen sink. He'd cleaned the cereal mess, stowed away the sofabed, and rolled up the sleeping bag. The bag and pillow sat on the couch along with several southwestern-patterned cushions. A local radio station played in the background instead of the TV sports.

"You look different," he said as he draped the cloth over the faucet and smiled over his shoulder.

"Aspirin works wonders."

"That's why they call it the miracle drug." He offered her a plate of buttered toast from the counter. "Hungry?"

Her stomach rumbled, and his eyebrows lifted.

"I'm taking that as a yes," he said, and Claire's heart softened. He was the nicest guy she'd ever met.

"I'm starving. Thank you." She picked up the top slice and sunk her teeth into the warm toast.

Ridge refilled her coffee. He had barely touched his mug, but she welcomed the infusion of caffeine to combat lingering cobwebs.

She drank the hot brew between bites of her second slice. Beside her at the counter, Ridge ate the other two pieces of toast.

His gaze flickered over her face. "You didn't have to pretty up for me, you know."

"Well, I couldn't have you confusing me with one of your corpses."

He laughed. "That wouldn't happen. You're a natural beauty, Claire." He tapped her nose, and sensual warmth pooled in her veins.

It's a simple nose-tap, she told herself. *Relax*. But the warmth progressed to a sizzling heat. Did he feel it too?

She hadn't dated since April. Not a long dry spell. But the last guy had been the opposite of easy-going Ridge Pederson. Not only in personality, but in looks and age. She usually dated serious-minded guys two to five years older. Would her three years matter to Ridge long-term?

She resisted giving her head a shake. Why was she thinking about their future?

The glimmer in his eyes suggested she needn't worry about their smallish age difference. He set his coffee mug on the counter.

"Ready to see Fargone?" he asked.

He adored that snake. "Is he poisonous?"

"Nah. Ball pythons kill by constriction."

"Charming. How long is he?"

"Three feet. He's still growing. He might reach five feet."

"That's reassuring."

Ridge chuckled. "Handled correctly, Fargone is harmless. Most snakes are nocturnal. Far is no exception. He's probably curled in his hiding cave."

Claire voiced her last objection. "Should we disturb him?"

Ridge rubbed her shoulder. The arousing tingle radiated through the flannel robe, and her heart raced.

Ridge smiled. "It's okay," he said quietly. "Far likes me. I take him out of his tank every day. You can handle him. Want to try?"

That would be a no. "How about *you* handle the snake, and I'll watch?"

"You'll watch, huh?"

Her cheeks warmed, but she liked Ridge's flirting. He was fun. And ambitious, with plans for his future.

"Don't get excited," she said, although she wouldn't mind if he did. "I meant your dad's snake." She smirked. "*Again.*"

He grinned. "Got it."

She battled the urge to fan herself. He was so handsome. She might hyperventilate.

She put down her mug. Ridge's palm settled on

her spine as he directed her to the second bedroom. Claire recognized the apartment layout from visiting Lacey.

"Which floor is this?" she asked.

"The second."

"My friend Lacey DeMarco lives two floors above your dad. She uses the spare bedroom as her design studio."

"What does she design?"

"Lingerie. She made my baby dolls." Claire touched the bodice of her outfit. Last night, she'd donned the sexy nightwear intending to seduce the image in Ridge's stripping ad—her lowest point since college. Now she realized he was so much more than the six-pack-equipped hottie who'd hip-thrusted his way down to a leather G-string during Tania's bachelorette party. He took care of his father's snake, he maintained a relationship with a mother who'd abandoned him, and he attended medical school. Check, check, and check.

"Lacey is very talented," Ridge said, his hand circling on Claire's lower back.

He opened the door to the snake room then flicked on a low-wattage light. A computer desk sat against the right wall. A rolling rack of stripping costumes flanked the left. Claire spied a sailor suit and a pirate costume. *Ahoy!*

She forced her gaze ahead. A four-foot-wide reptile tank sat on a sturdy-looking stand beneath the blind-drawn window.

Ridge clasped her hand and led her to the tank, which contained wood shavings, a water dish, a lamp Ridge described as a heat dome, plus various hiding and climbing structures.

Claire hung back while he hunkered on his heels and peered into the tank.

"I see Far." Ridge unlatched the lid and lifted a hiding cave. He grasped the snake by its middle, supporting the creature with his forearm. A moment later, he stood and presented the snake.

Claire let out a soft squeak. The reptile coiled into a ball. An empty depression marred Fargone's head where the poor thing had lost an eye. The healthy eye glistened.

The snake relaxed, curling around Ridge's forearm. He balanced the python against his chest and whispered, "Want to touch him?"

"I'll startle him," Claire whispered back. Poor Fargone, the one-eyed snake. She shouldn't have judged him.

"You won't bother him. Balls have excellent dispositions. And Far is docile after living with my dad for months."

Claire smiled. "Balls?" Was she twelve?

"You make me wanna go there."

"Am I the only woman you tease like this?" *Why had she said that?*

"You are now," he responded, his gaze drifting to the snake. "But if you're scared, it's best not to touch Far. If he gets stressed, he might not eat tonight."

"We can't have that." *Sorry, fridge mouse. You're already a goner.*

Ridge sat cross-legged on the floor. He positioned the snake around his neck and murmured to the creature as Fargone's three-foot-long body undulated in his hands. Claire's insides turned as gooey as a bag of roasted marshmallows. Was there anything sexier than this half-naked man caring for a cold-blooded reptile?

Only if he handled *her* with such care.

Continuing to hang back, she whispered, "I'm sorry I misjudged you, Ridge."

He looked up. "Are you judging me now?"

"Yes. And I think you're incredible."

He smiled. "What do you do for work?" He didn't

pressure her to sit or touch the snake. His gaze remained on her face, his head tilting as he listened.

"Have you heard of Clemmons Consulting?" she asked.

"It doesn't ring a bell. Are they local?"

She nodded. "They're a venture capital group in downtown Seattle. They specialize in helping small businesses. I'm an executive assistant to a founder. When I showed him Lacey's designs, he agreed to introduce her to his team."

"Wow. That was nice of you."

"Lacey deserves the chance to follow her dreams."

"What are *your* dreams, Claire?" Ridge removed the snake from around his neck and let the creature curl on his forearm again.

Claire toyed with the robe sash. She rarely opened up to men right away, but Ridge had shared his feelings about his mom. He would understand her wish for a normal family life, if such a thing existed.

"In a minute," she said, kneeling beside him. The robe puddled on the wood laminate floor. "I want to touch Fargone first." She rolled up the housecoat sleeves.

"You're fearless," Ridge whispered. He secured the ball python with both hands.

Claire held her breath and drifted a fingertip along the creature's scales. "He feels silky-smooth," she whispered. Not slimy or sticky, like she'd feared.

She touched Fargone again. The snake's head moved away.

"I enjoy my job," she said, looking at Ridge. "Work doesn't drive me, though. I don't have a calling or a passion. Not the way you must, attending medical school. I can't imagine not contributing financially when I get married. But the thing I want most is a family. Two parents and a couple of kids." She hesitated. "You mentioned your mom leaving. I know how you feel. In my case, it was my biological father who took off."

"What happened?" Concern resonated in Ridge's tone as the snake wove between his splayed fingers.

"He wasn't ready to become a dad, I guess." Claire shrugged off the sadness, although some deep-rooted emotion from childhood lingered and probably always would. "He left when I was one. My mom raised my older sister and me alone for a few years."

Ridge shook his head. "I'm sorry, Claire. Did he ever come back?"

"No." She looked away a moment. "Unlike your mom, he didn't grow into the idea of parenthood. For the longest time, I blamed myself. It makes no sense, considering I was a baby when he left, but it felt like I did something wrong. Maybe I cried too much or kept him up at night. Squalling baby Claire must have *made* him leave." She placed a hand on her upper chest. "My mom was great. We discussed my dad whenever I or my sister needed. In the end, I realized his absence from our lives was his failing, not ours."

"You got that right. Your mom sounds incredible."

"She's awesome." Claire reached out to stroke Fargone again. She didn't cringe as the snake's head moved toward her hand. Ridge had the creature under control. "The frustrating part is that for all we know, our bio-dad fell off a cliff somewhere. Support payments stopped two years after he left. By then, our mom had met her second husband, so she was just as happy not to keep tracking down our birth father. Neil—my stepdad—adopted my sister and me. I wasn't born a Merriweather."

"What's your birth name?"

"Claire Smith. I know, boring."

"Merriweather has more flair," Ridge observed.

"I don't remember a lot about my bio-dad. My mom gave me photos when I was younger. After a while, I filed them away. In my heart, Neil is my father."

"Still. Not knowing where your bio-dad is sounds rough." Ridge supported Fargone's body while the snake moved.

Claire nodded. "It hurts that he dropped out of our lives that way. For years, I felt incredibly insecure. My sister and I have a little brother from Neil and my mom, and he's great. *They're* my family. I want the same sense of security for my own kids someday."

"I get it." Ridge's brown eyes warmed. "Family is more about how a group of people treats each other than if they're related by blood."

"I agree. You're smart for someone so young."

"And you're old?"

"I'm twenty-seven."

He grinned. "I bet you could teach me a few things."

"Maybe I already have." Her heart pounded against her ribs. "Are you sure we didn't kiss last night?"

"Only in my dreams. You were drunk, and I'm not a creep." Moving slowly, he got up and unwound the snake.

Claire stood. She tidied her robe as Ridge placed the snake on top of a hiding cave in the tank. Ridge secured the lid on the glass enclosure, and Fargone slipped into the cave.

Ridge stepped toward her. "So." He slid his hands along her forearms. "Where were we?"

"Establishing that I'm not drunk now," she whispered.

His gaze dropped to her cleavage. "You're half-dressed."

"Look who's talking." She glided her fingers over his muscular chest. "If you can restrain yourself from taking things beyond a kiss right now, so can I." Jumping his bones while a hangover lurked was not in her plans.

"God, Claire." Voice rough, he gathered her into a snug embrace. She curled her arms around his waist and looked up. Eyes as dark as espresso beans gazed down at her. His growing erection made itself known against the bathrobe covering her belly. "Ignore that."

"I'll try."

He lowered his lips to hers. The kiss began slow

and sweet. Her skin hummed and her nipples tightened as his tongue skimmed over her lips. The kiss deepened, and her pulse fluttered.

How had this happened to her? The girl the popular kids in high school had called Quiet Claire hungered to throw caution aside, to forget what her friends might think about her hooking up with the hot guy from the bachelorette party, and go for it with Ridge. Physically. Emotionally. In every way.

With one last tender caress of her mouth, he brushed her hair back from her face. "You have somewhere to be," he murmured.

She nodded. "The dress fitting." She was Tania's maid of honor. She couldn't disappoint her best friend. "Alicia is waiting for me. We were supposed to drive to Belltown together."

"I'll take you. We can go for lunch afterward."

Claire sighed. "Sounds wonderful. I need to pick up my stuff from Alicia's. I brought a change of clothes for today."

"Why not shower here? I'll get dressed and grab your stuff. I need to put a load into the wash anyway."

Claire's cheeks burned. "Oh, no. Your laundry basket is still downstairs? I'm sorry."

"Don't be." He brushed her chin with his thumb. "I'll never regret meeting you, Claire."

"*I'll* never regret throwing myself at you."

"I'll never regret catching you."

"I'll never regret what will happen later tonight."

"Will?" he asked, gaze hopeful.

"Definitely."

He kissed her. "No regrets."

Chapter Five

Ridge dumped detergent into the washing machine closest to where he'd met Claire. With a smile on his face, he left the laundry and rode the elevator to the fourth floor.

Had he really volunteered his free Saturday to driving a woman to a dress fitting? Claire intrigued him on multiple levels. He didn't care if her promise of "later tonight" materialized. Well, he cared. He *was* a guy. But he wanted to share more than sex with Claire. Despite only knowing her for a few hours, their connection electrified him.

The elevator dinged. He exited the stall and headed toward Alicia Maxwell's apartment. A new chalkboard message on the door announced:

Cupcake emergency! Sorry, C. Meet you at the salon. L has your stuff.

Ridge frowned. Cupcake emergency? What was that about?

He knocked on the door across the hall, where Claire had said Lacey lived. The fair-haired woman from last night's party answered, wearing jeans and a rumpled top. A yawning dachshund stretched behind her bare feet.

Ridge waved. "Hey, there. Lacey? I'm Ridge Pederson. The dancer from the party."

Tiny lines of tiredness feathered around Lacey's eyes. Apparently, Claire wasn't the only party guest who'd enjoyed a late night.

"The party at Alicia Maxwell's apartment," he clarified, pointing across the hall.

"Ridge." Lacey nodded. "You're Claire's friend. Sorry. I didn't recognize you without your costume." The dog's nose poked between her shins. She glanced down at the animal. "Uh-uh, Spats," she admonished in a melodic voice. "No escaping." She looked at Ridge. "I'm watching him for Alicia." She peered down at the dog again. "And he'd better not steal my lingerie samples this time."

"Uh, okay." Ridge wiped his hands on the rear of his jeans. Had the dog stolen Lacey's samples another time? "The note on Alicia's door says you have Claire's stuff. Claire sent me for a duffel bag."

"Where is Claire now?"

"Taking a shower at my place."

Lacey's gaze narrowed. "Is she in one piece?"

"What?" Ridge shook his head. "Yes, she's in one piece. I'm not an axe-murderer, if that's what you mean. Claire had too much to drink last night, but she slept it off."

"While wearing the baby dolls I made for her, I hope. Unless she slept it off naked?"

What the hell? "*Yes*, she wore the baby dolls."

"Good." Lacey's gaze roamed over him. "Sorry, Ridge, but you had some sexy moves at the party."

"I'm a dancer. We're supposed to have moves." He didn't owe this woman further explanation.

Lacey nodded. "One minute." Backing up with the dog between her ankles, she closed the door. When it opened again, muffled barking carried from another room. "Sorry about the noise. Spats doesn't understand why he can't go back to Alicia's." She handed Ridge a small duffel bag. "Everything is in there. Claire's clothes from the bachelorette party, a change for today, plus her purse and shoes. Please make sure she doesn't forget the purple sandals for the dress fitting. Was she wearing them last night? Alicia couldn't find them."

Ridge nodded. "The sandals are in my living room."

"Great. Claire needs to take them to the salon. They match her gown." Lacey held up a finger. "She needs to check her phone. It's rung ten times in the last hour, and I don't know her passcode."

"Gotcha."

Lacey closed the door an inch. "Have her text me within the next five minutes. Even better, she should call. I want to hear her tell me she's okay."

"You'll receive her call soon."

Lacey stared him in the eyes. "You treat her right."

He stepped back. "I intend to."

"Don't let your hot dancing turn her head. She deserves the best."

"Come on, Lacey. You don't know me. I wouldn't hurt Claire. I haven't."

Lacey's chin lifted. "A girl can't be too careful."

"You're right. I understand."

She smiled. "Okay. You passed my test. Have a great day!" The door shut.

Ridge shook his head and returned to the second floor. Lacey had ripped into him like a mother toting a shotgun. Claire's friends stood up for and defended each other. She had family in more than one way. He respected that.

As he entered his dad's place, Claire came out of the bathroom, her hair wrapped in a towel and his robe tied around her curves. She'd rinsed the makeup off her face, and faint shadows dusted the delicate skin beneath her eyes. She was the sexiest thing he'd ever seen.

He gave her the duffel bag. "Here you go."

"Thanks. Did you talk to Alicia?"

"No. She wasn't home. Something about cupcakes. She wants you to meet her at the salon. Good thing you have a ride." He winked.

"I'll say. Thanks so much. I hope nothing is wrong at her shop. Wait. If Alicia's not home, how did you get my stuff?"

"Lacey had the duffel. She said your phone keeps ringing. She wants you to call her. To make sure I haven't cut you up and fed you to Fargone."

Claire chuckled, unzipping the duffel bag and locating her phone.

They walked to the couch. Claire checked in with Lacey before scanning her messages. Her eyes widened. "Yikes. Text city." As if on cue, the phone rang. "It's Tania," Claire said, glancing at the notification. She put the phone to her ear.

A female voice echoed from the speaker. Claire's face whitened.

"What's wrong?" Ridge whispered, massaging her shoulder.

She lowered the phone to her hip. "I'm late. Tania's mom changed the appointment time!" The wrapped towel tilted on her head.

Tania's voice carried from the phone. "Claire, my dress is awful! It just hangs on me. I look like a shrunken mermaid! Where are you?" A pause ensued. "Mom!"

A second female voice commandeered the phone. "Claire Merriweather, tardiness does not befit a maid of honor. My dear, you are unreliable."

Claire gasped and slapped the phone back against her ear. "The fitting is at twelve, Mrs. H. Tania confirmed the time with me last night." The towel unraveled and tumbled to the floor.

Ridge retrieved the damp towel and tossed it onto the couch. His hand bumped Claire's calf, and the phone sprang off her ear again.

Tania's mom's voice hissed over the speaker. "Claire Merriweather, thanks to you and those monster-sized drinks, Tania was *intoxicated*. She confirmed the wrong time. You should have checked with me. How many times have I told you?"

Claire spoke into the phone. "I'm sorry for the misunderstanding, Mrs. H. I'll get there as soon as I can." Features twisting, she disconnected.

Ridge touched her shoulders and gazed into her worried green eyes. "Just how deep is this doo-doo?"

"Grand Canyon deep," she wailed.

"Aw, Claire." He gathered her into his arms and stroked her wet hair.

Chapter Six

The rumbling of Ridge's old motorcycle reverberated throughout Claire's body as he maneuvered the noisy machine into the last parking spot near Bettina's Bridal Couture. Claire peeled her fingertips off his soft leather vest. Earlier, she hadn't realized his offer of a ride would require her to tug on a helmet over her soggy hair. Now, not only had they made decent time, but she'd experienced the thrill of her first motorcycle ride.

Ridge planted a booted foot on the pavement and turned off the ignition.

"Can I take off my helmet?" Claire asked.

He flipped up his visor. "It's safer to wait until you've dismounted. I'll steady the bike." He clasped the handles. "Balance one foot on the peg," he advised, pressing both boots on the pavement. "Swing your other leg over the seat. Careful not to touch the hot exhaust pipe."

The motorcycle barely wobbled as Claire followed his directions. Stepping onto the busy Belltown sidewalk, she hauled off the protective gear while he set the kickstand and dismounted. His dark gaze traipsed over her face, and his lips curled into a sexy grin.

"What?" Claire glimpsed her reflection in a side mirror. "Crap!" After getting chewed out by Mrs. H., she hadn't wanted to waste time blow-drying her hair. As a result, several tangled waves plastered her skull. "I look like a drowned swamp rat."

He laughed. "You're cute." He took off his helmet and hung it on a handle.

"Cute?" Was he farsighted?

"That's what I said."

She refused to burst his first-day-together bubble. "Hold this." She thrust her helmet into his hands and ran to the rear of the bike. A bungee cord secured her purse to a chrome carrier rack. After a glance here and a twist there, she yanked off the purse and pawed through the contents. No comb! No hairbrush!

Ridge slung her helmet over the second bike

handle. He squeezed her arm over her windblown jacket. "I'll go in with you."

"You don't want to do that," she warned. Really, he was too much. Too kind and sweet. Too hot and handsome. Setting her purse on the seat, she hunched in front of the side mirror and tidied her matted mop.

"It's my fault you're late," Ridge said, raking his fingers through his thick locks. His bangs stood up in sexy spikes. "Now we both have helmet head."

Claire giggled. She liked him *so much*. Twenty-four hours ago, she hadn't imagined they might spend the afternoon together.

Then there was tonight. Or was she moving too fast?

She ached to sky-dive out of her comfort zone with Ridge. Would sleeping together at this early stage of their relationship sabotage their chances for long-term? As the day had unfolded, she'd realized Ridge Pederson wasn't a cookie to swallow in two bites. He deserved her full attention. *They* deserved to take their time.

She nibbled her lip. "Isn't there someplace you'd rather be?" Most guys would rather chew sawdust than attend a dress fitting.

"Ashamed of me?" he asked.

"Never."

"Then let me come in with you. There's a wild-ness in your eyes, Claire, as if you're about to walk the plank. That can't be healthy."

"Tania's mom has that effect on people," Claire said dryly. "And I love Tania, but she's been super-stressed about wedding stuff. Her mom's anxiety must be rubbing off on her."

Ridge nodded. "So let her mom see you walking in with the stripper from the party. The woman's head will explode."

Claire smiled. "How will Mrs. H. know you're the stripper?"

His right shoulder lifted. "Ten-to-one, someone will fill her in."

Claire's heart fluttered as rapidly as humming-bird wings. She was falling hard for this guy. "Okay."

She took her purse, and he carried the helmets. They entered the salon featuring six private dressing suites and a central runway. Ridge's motorcycle boots clomped on the fashionably worn hardwood.

Claire guided him toward a white reception desk. A shiver raced up her spine as he placed a hand on the small of her back.

"The Hoyt-Whitaker wedding," Claire said to the receptionist. "I'm the maid of honor."

The woman eyed Ridge as if he were a slab of meat. Or a bag of cookies. He didn't reward the receptionist's slow and awkward appraisal of his stellar attributes with a single glance, Claire noted.

"Hoyt-Whitaker," he repeated, gesturing a hand at the woman. "Maid of honor? Hello?"

The receptionist tapped a long fingernail against her desk. "This way, please." She rose and led them deep into the building. In the halls, stylists hustled back and forth, collecting gowns for their assigned brides.

The receptionist opened a door into a room overflowing with Tania's group and shut Claire and Ridge inside pure chaos.

Ridge's gaze widened. "Holy X-ray results. This place is busier than an ER."

"Except no one's life is in danger," Claire said. "Yet." She surveyed the scene. Janie, Alicia, and Tania's two younger sisters surrounded the bride-to-be in front of a lighted three-way mirror. Each bridesmaid wore a matching dress style in varying colors of fuchsia, coral, goldenrod, and tangerine. A red-faced Mrs. Hoyt, gussied up in a tailored skirt suit, attempted to corral Teacup, Tania's miniature Yorkshire Terrier. Teacup's rhinestone barrette bounced as the dog yipped at the hem of Tania's gorgeous mermaid-style wedding gown.

Tania sobbed, her face in her hands. "It's all wrong! It's all wrong! It's all wrong!"

"This is wild," Ridge whispered.

"*This* is estrogen overload." Claire sat him on a velvet bench near the door. He placed the motor-cycle helmets on the floor, and she murmured, "My advice? Don't breathe a word." Tossing her purse and jacket onto the bench, she arrowed for her best friend.

Tania whirled around. "Claire! You're here. Thank God. I need your advice." Tania clutched her gown.

Tania's mom snatched up Teacup. The woman's gaze winged to Ridge. "Who's this?"

"My friend, Ridge," Claire told Mrs. H. "He's my ride."

Tania's eyes rounded. "The stripper from my party? Go, Claire!"

Mrs. H. gaped. "You brought a stripper to my baby's fitting?" Teacup squirmed in the woman's arms.

Tania's youngest sister said to the middle, "No wonder they didn't invite us to the second shower. It was a tacky-fest."

Janie glared at the pair. "Last night's event was for Tania's friends. Same with the bachelorette party afterward."

The sisters gasped. "That's rude," the middle Hoyt said.

"We needed to let off some steam," Claire told them. Sometimes Tania's sisters acted as if *they* were the ones getting married.

Mrs. H. flung up a hand. "None of that matters now." Clutching Teacup, she strode toward Claire. Alicia lifted the skirt of her dress and intercepted the woman. Tania's mom adjusted course and marched toward Ridge. He straightened on the bench.

Alicia touched Claire's arm. "I'm sorry I needed to cancel your ride. There was a mixup with the ingredients for tonight's catering job. It was my fault. I had to redo the cupcakes."

"Three hundred of them?" Claire whispered. "Alicia, that's awful."

Mrs. Hoyt dumped a wriggling Teacup onto Ridge's lap. "Make yourself useful." She turned back around, facing Claire.

Ridge's jaw clenched, but he held the dog.

Claire shot him a glance. "Thank you," she mouthed.

Mrs. H. scrutinized Claire from head to toe. "Claire Merriweather, where are your sandals?"

The blood drained from Claire's face. "Shit— shoot." In her hurry to get to the salon, she hadn't brought her wedding shoes, which Mrs. H. had been kind enough to buy. At the apartment, upon glimpsing the motorcycle helmets and realizing she was in for yet another new experience with Ridge, she hadn't spared the sandals a second thought.

But she wasn't eight years old. She wouldn't allow Mrs. H. to intimidate her. Or to treat Ridge like garbage.

She squared her shoulders. "I forgot the sandals in Ridge's apartment. I'm sorry."

Alicia's forehead wrinkled. "But I gave your stuff to Lacey."

"That's where Ridge picked up my duffel bag," Claire said. "While I showered, which explains the sad state of my hair."

Noni, the youngest Hoyt, sneered. "You showered with a stripper?"

Claire scowled at her. "Not that it's any of your business, but no." She would rectify the situation soon enough, if Ridge still wanted to explore their attraction after this embarrassing experience.

Mrs. H. produced a long-suffering sigh. "You

forgot the sandals. How will we decide the proper length to hem your dress?" She beckoned a finger at a hovering stylist. "Alberta? Plan B."

Alberta selected a coral gown from a rack and pressed the dress into Claire's hands. The shiny fabric scrunched.

"Into the dressing room with you now, Claire," Mrs. H. said. "And please hurry. You can use Tami's sandals for the fitting." She snapped her fingers at her middle daughter. Tami wrenched off her tangerine footwear and relinquished the pair.

Claire's mind spun. She stared at the sandals and substitute dress in her hands. "But my dress is purple."

"Not anymore." Mrs. H.'s gaze swept over Claire's hourglass figure. "You were supposed to lose ten pounds for the wedding, not gain five." The woman flicked a hand at Claire's hair. "No highlights, I see."

Claire stuck her nose in the air. "And none will be forthcoming."

Face hot, she ducked into a dressing room. Ridge called out her name, but she slammed shut the flimsy door.

She couldn't face him. She couldn't face any of them.

But she had to.

As she changed at warp speed, the reflection of the ruffled coral dress lent her complexion a sallow cast. The style mismatched the others to an insulting degree. The garment had multiple layers and no waist! The yards of fabric could easily clothe Tania, Claire, *and* Tania's mom.

Claire clomped back into the salon. "This damn dress is three sizes too big."

Tania's face crumpled. "Now you know my problem. I lost too much weight."

"And I lost five pounds," Claire informed Tania's mom. "I didn't gain an ounce."

Mrs. H. soothed her daughter. "There, there, Tania, sweetheart," she murmured. "We'll have your gown taken in a half-inch on either side. It'll be perfect."

A tear trickled down Tania's cheek. "What about Claire? She loves purple. My maid of honor deserves a special color."

Claire's heart pinched. This wedding wasn't about *her*.

She wrapped her arms around her best friend. The fabric of their dresses crinkled. "Tania, I'm sorry I was late. Your mom is right about your gown. It needs tailoring, that's all. And I'll wear whatever you want."

A sharp whistle pierced the air. Claire glanced around as Ridge strode toward Tania's mom. He deposited Teacup back into the woman's arms.

"You," he said to Mrs. H., "are a piece of work."

"Well," Mrs. H. responded. "I'm not the one who went crawling after a stripper."

Ridge's expression hardened. "Claire did not crawl after me. She had too much to drink, and I took care of her. Which is more than I can say for..." He pointed at Alicia. "You."

Alicia gasped. "Me?"

He nodded. "The party was at your apartment. You let Claire play bartender the whole evening. Didn't you pay attention to the alcohol your guests were consuming? But you left her alone."

Alicia stared at the floor. "I know it sounds bad. I thought she'd fall asleep right away."

"*Alone*," Ridge repeated. He glared at Tania. "You need to dial it down."

"Hold on," Claire told him. These women were her friends.

"I can't hold on," he argued. "The woman I met last night goes after what she wants. The woman I thought I was getting to know today stands up for herself. Claire, you're beautiful. You're strong. And you're worth a hell of a lot more consideration than your friends are giving you here today. If you want to escape this foolishness, I'll be at the bike." He strode to the bench, grabbed both helmets, and disappeared out the door.

Chapter Seven

Dead silence fell over the women. Claire glanced around the dressing suite as the echoing of Ridge's motorcycle boots thudded in the hallway.

Mrs. H. patted Teacup's head. "That didn't go over well." She looked at Claire. "If we take in the coral six inches, your new dress will fit very nice. The ruffles are delightful."

Claire gritted her teeth. "The ruffles make me look like a giant doll cake. I can fit the purple."

Mrs. H. exhaled. "Maybe so, dear. I was thinking a unique *style* for the maid of honor would help you stand out."

Tania stepped between Claire and Mrs. Hoyt. "Claire is wearing the purple," Tania stated with authority. "It's my wedding, so it's my say." She clasped Claire's hand. "The purple looks gorgeous on you, and our friendship is golden to me." She smiled. "Now, go after Ridge. It's obvious he's into you, and the glow in your eyes says you think he's all kinds of wonderful."

Any glow radiating from Claire's eyes right now was meant to laser a hole in Tania's mom, but she refrained from correcting her oldest and dearest friend.

"You and I can hem the purple dress tomorrow," Tania continued, rubbing Claire's arm. "If that works for you. We'll alter your dress together, like the best buds we are."

Claire's chest warmed. "That sounds perfect, Tania. Thank you."

The other bridesmaids and the stylist murmured their approval.

Mrs. H. looked at Claire. "It's true about Ridge, dear. He appeared besotted. He had the nerve to confront me, and that's something. Please accept my apologies. And extend them to him as well?"

Claire nodded. Two years of wedding planning had taken a toll on everyone. But this latest catastrophe would not destroy her chances with Ridge.

She grabbed her jacket and purse off the bench and hustled out the door.

"The dress!" the stylist called.

"My shoes!" Tami cried.

Claire kept walking, the ruffles of the ugly coral dress rustling as she pulled on her jacket.

Mrs. Hoyt's voice carried from the suite. "Hush, Tams. Claire will return your sandals tomorrow. And Alberta? That dress! I asked for the next size up, not a tent."

Claire navigated her way past the busy stylists and the gawking receptionist. Outside, Ridge straddled the roaring motorcycle at the curb. The helmets sat on the sidewalk near his right boot.

Claire strapped her purse onto the carrier at the back of the bike before stepping beside Ridge. She swept her fingers along his muscular biceps. "Sorry about that zoo. Tania's mom sends her apologies." Claire offered a small smile. "Now you know why men just like to show up for weddings. Planning them is the pits."

An amused glint lit his brown eyes. "You came after me wearing that dress?"

"I'd run after you naked. The wedding is two weeks away. The stress is weighing on Tania." Claire waited a beat. "We've been best friends forever. Tania is sweet. And her mom doesn't intimidate me anymore." *Claire* bore responsibility for how she perceived herself. Not her deadbeat biological father. Not the kids from high school. And not Tania's mom.

"The mom is a winner," Ridge observed.

Claire needed him to understand. "I'm not trying to excuse her behavior, but her husband split when the girls were little. She became a control freak."

"Hey, I get it. Nobody's perfect. I've been told my dick's too long."

Claire burst out laughing.

"I'm serious." He rested a hand on her cheek. "The last girl found *it* intimidating. And she hasn't been around for a long time, Claire."

Claire held her breath. "Then I look forward to learning about your dick myself." She paused. "After a few dates."

"No more definitely tonight?"

"I can't have you thinking I'm only after you for your body."

"I can't have you thinking I'm only after you for your mind." He grinned. "I have no problem waiting." Cupping her face, he kissed her, long and soulful, as the motorcycle thundered between them. He retrieved the helmets and handed her the smaller one. "Where are we heading?"

"To my place, so I can change. Then you owe me lunch."

He chuckled. "I like your take-charge side."

"Good. So do I."

He tapped the passenger seat. "Hop on."

Claire donned the helmet, climbed up behind him in the coral dress, and tucked the ruffles around her thighs. Heart racing, she scooped her arms around his waist. "Let's go!"

Natural light flooded the living room in Claire's expansive apartment. Ridge considered the contemporary dining set and the L-shaped sofa occupying a corner. Tasteful prints decorated the walls, and large plants flanked a floor-to-ceiling bookcase. His stomach clenched. Claire's place was larger and several degrees classier than the space he shared with two medical students. Was she out of his league?

"Nice digs," he said, pretending the question of whether they really suited each other wasn't hitting him in the solar plexus. "Want to be my sugar mama?"

She folded her jacket over an armchair. The hem

of the baggy bridesmaid dress swirled around her legs. "My stepdad encouraged my sister and me to invest when we each turned twenty-one," she replied in a tone implying her accomplishments weren't a big deal. "Neil didn't want us to feel financially obligated to anyone."

Ridge nodded. That made sense.

"Because of what your mom went through with your bio-dad?" he asked.

"Yeah. Plus, Neil works in the field. He talked about his job a lot as we grew up. Taking his advice felt like second nature. I got lucky, and this place is the result."

"You own instead of renting?" Ridge whistled. "I'm impressed."

"Now we're even," Claire murmured, sliding him a seductive glance as she stepped within an inch of him. "I'm impressed with you, and you're impressed with me."

His concerns evaporated. He felt at home with Claire. Strange as it might seem during their first day together, he also felt at home in her apartment. It looked polished, but not frilly. He imagined spending evenings on the couch with Claire's head nestled against his chest and his arms encircling her curvy body. They'd stream a movie while sharing pizza or Chinese food or a nutritious meal whipped up in the kitchen. Then they'd do what came naturally following a movie and chilling....

Claire stretched up on tiptoe and brushed a lock of hair off his forehead. "What are you thinking about?" she whispered.

"Our future," he admitted.

Her eyes sparkled. "Same."

He pulled her into a close embrace. "Is it weird to feel so connected to you already?" he whispered against her temple.

"I don't care if it is." Her hands slid beneath his leather motorcycle vest and ran over his T-shirt. "Our lunch needs to wait," she said, voice sultry.

He gazed at her face. "Oh, really?" Ten minutes ago, they'd bought takeout from a bagels and burritos shop around the corner. The bag and motorcycle helmets sat on the dining table.

"Yes." Claire smiled. "I said I needed to change before lunch. Remember?"

Ridge was lucky he remembered his name while holding this incredible woman. "Yeah."

She plucked the neckline of the ruffled dress. "Well...I'm changing out of Plan B—as Tania's mom called this horrible outfit. If it's okay with you,

Ridge," Claire said softly, "I'm jumping straight to Plan C."

"Plan C?" He didn't recall a Plan C.

Her lips pursed. "Plan C as in Plan Claire. I guess it's Plan CR, for Claire and Ridge. Or Plan RC, for Ridge and Claire."

He planted a kiss on her pouty mouth. "Either sounds better than Cridge."

"Then I choose RC. And the plan begins with you helping me out of this dress." She motioned behind her neck. "I struggled with the zipper while you dealt with the helmets and food. It's stuck. Back at the salon, I yanked on it like I was reeling in a whale. I must've wrecked it." Turning around, she lifted her hair. "Do you mind?"

He swallowed, his throat tight with need. "In what world would I mind?"

She glanced over her shoulder, and her dark eyelashes fluttered. "In the one where I keep changing *my* mind about whether we're indulging in a round of afternoon delight, as the old folks say."

"Afternoon delight?" Ridge echoed. His one-eyed snake hardened in his jeans. "Claire," he whispered. "Are you sure?" He located the tiny zipper.

Her head lolled sexily on his shoulder. "Yes."

His erection swelled, and he fumbled with the

zipper tab. "Why do they make these things too small for a guy's fingers?" His excitement mounted.

"So you'll rip the fabric and need to buy a replacement dress," she responded with a confident shrug.

"Worth it," Ridge murmured, growing harder. He scrutinized the zipper tab and tugged. To no avail. He swore. "This thing is good and stuck. I feel like a kid caught with my fingers in a candy jar."

A sigh drifted from her mouth. "You can dip your fingers in my candy jar."

Groaning, he pressed a kiss to her warm shoulder. "I hope you have scissors. We're gonna need them in another minute." He grabbed the dress on either side of the zipper and wrenched. The shiny fabric tore from the billowing neckline to her armpits. "This dress has seen better days," he mumbled.

"It doesn't matter," Claire said in a dreamy voice. "This nightmare of a gown is on Mrs. H.'s tab. And her conscience." Claire faced him and glided the destroyed dress off her shoulders. A lacy bra exposed her cleavage. She twisted his T-shirt in a fist. "To the bedroom, my good doctor," she murmured, hauling him along as she paced backward toward an open door.

He spotted the bed. "*Future* doctor," he reminded her for some inexplicable reason.

"To the bed, my good future doctor, then."

They reached the bed. Ridge curled his hands around her waist and split the dress down to her hips. The fabric sagged.

"Scissors no longer required," he whispered.

She collapsed onto the mattress, taking him and yards of fabric with her. She shoved his vest off his shoulders. "I'm getting impatient, my hot and sexy future doctor."

An emotion far too intense for Day One expanded in his chest. This woman had captivated him. There was no other explanation, he realized as lust blazed in his veins. He wanted nothing more than to bunch the ruffled dress at her waist, rip off her panties, and bury himself inside her softness. *Right now*. But something she'd said in the laundry room required his attention.

Stepping back, he pulled off his T-shirt and unlaced his boots. "You're the sexiest woman I've ever been with." He tucked his socks into the boots on the far side of her nightstand.

Her gaze flew over his naked chest. "And you're steaming hot." Sitting cross-legged on the bedcovers, she heaved up the tattered dress until the shiny fabric covered her face. She coughed. "I might smother to death. Help me, my steaming hot good future doctor."

Chuckling, Ridge swept his hands over her ribs and extricated her from the demolished gown. He wadded the dress into a ball and chucked the bundle across the room.

"That's going in the garbage," he said, meeting her heated gaze for a sexually charged moment. He savored a leisurely journey of her shape in a matching bra and panties set. Need chewed his gut, and he scrubbed a hand on his jaw. "Claire, before we do this, I gotta say something."

"What is it?"

"I hated what Tania's mom said about your hair and your beautiful body back at the salon. And last night in the laundry, you said—" He sucked in a breath. Would reminding her of her vulnerability cut short their first time together?

Claire blinked. "In the laundry?" she parroted. "Ridge, let's drag everything out into the open. What other dumb things did I say or do last night?"

"Let me put it this way. You didn't pay yourself a compliment. And I want to set the record straight, honey. You were dead wrong."

Chapter Eight

Heat singed Claire's neck. She pinched her nose. "Did I call myself fat?" she asked, groaning when Ridge nodded.

Way to go, Claire. Practically jump into the man's arms in the frigging laundry while tearing a hundred-foot-wide hole in your self-confidence.

She balanced on her knees on the mattress and moved to the edge of the bed, dressed only in her bra and panties. The roundness of her hips, her soft tummy, and her full breasts were on display in her elegant lingerie. Their gazes met.

"Sometimes I'm insecure," she half-whispered, searching Ridge's espresso-brown eyes. "Is that a problem? Because it's gonna happen from time to time. Ridge, if we're doing this—and by that I mean a relationship, not an afternoon one-off—I need to break it to you. I'm hardly a bone rack."

He frowned. "I don't want to make love with a bone rack." He gripped her shoulders. "I like what I see. Scratch that. I *love* what I see." His hungry gaze devoured her body, and a thrill coursed through her.

"Not into plastic skeletons?" she teased. "The contraptions most doctors keep in their offices don't turn you on?"

His eyebrows furrowed. Clare preferred the primal need burning in his gaze a moment ago.

"Please don't make light of this, honey."

"I'm not. But Ridge, when a woman has been called a 'chunky monkey' half her life, fears work into her psyche. They did for me, at any rate." She tugged in a breath. "I hope what I said last night hasn't blown our chances at a relationship." And he'd better not suggest they throw out their lunch of bagels and burritos and dash to the grocery store for celery and no-fat dip. Because Claire wanted him more than she'd wanted another man in her life. And then she wanted her cream-cheese-and-salted-cucumber bagel.

He shook his head. "You haven't blown anything."

"Not yet." Claire fondled his erection, encased in rough jeans. "Although maybe on our second date." She stroked his hardness. Arousal threaded throughout her body. Trying to appear studious, she murmured in her best sexy-scientist voice, "Hmm. I detect length. And...*oh, yes.*" She squeezed and stroked. "I detect magnificent girth."

He grinned. "Woman, you'll be the death of me."

"Your dick might be the death of me, but I'm up to the challenge. Are you?"

"I'll go slow," he growled, eyes closing as she moved her hand outside the denim.

"Don't you dare treat me like a fragile piece of glass." Claire dug a condom out of her nightstand drawer while Ridge unzipped and kicked off his jeans and underwear.

Heart pounding, she gawked at his erection as he rolled on the condom. Mamma Mia, he hadn't lied about his length!

"Okay, go a little slow at first," she suggested, trusting that she sounded daring and sensual and up for anything and everything with this extraordinary man. Adventurous lovemaking. A deep and enduring relationship. Whatever surprises life held in store, if she shared them all with Ridge.

She stood up on the rumpled bedcover and

whisked off her panties and bra. "I'm ready," she announced.

"I'll be the judge of that." He reached behind her knees, buckling her onto her butt and back.

"Oh!" Her breasts jiggled as he spread her legs, cupped her rear in his hands, and buried his face in the exact spot she needed him to be.

Inhaling her intimate scent, he parted her folds with his lips and tested her wetness with his fingers.

As he licked and sucked, his hands skipped up her ribs and captured her nipples. He rolled them between his fingertips while he feasted. Sensation ricocheted between her thighs.

She panted, clenching the bedcovers. Her hips arched, and her heart threatened to clamber out of her chest. "Ridge! Oh, no." She couldn't handle the exquisite tension. "I'm ready." She clutched his shoulders. "I need you inside me." Before she exploded into a million galaxies.

His head lifted. "Yum. It can happen twice, honey. Now and then again when I'm inside you. I know what I'm doing."

She didn't doubt his erotic prowess. She craved the ecstasy of his fingers and mouth between her legs. But for their first time, she wanted their bodies joined as intimately as possible. Face to face. Heart to heart.

A strong premonition swept over her. She wouldn't experience a first time making love with another man. Ridge was it for her.

She said on a soft murmur, "Not today. Get inside me."

"My fingers *are* inside you," he whispered, inching them in and out. "But if you insist..." He moved them away.

"Ridge!" She grabbed his hair. "I changed my mind." Again. But not about him being in her life. Never about him. "Stay there. I want to look at you."

"Do it," he whispered, gaze connecting with hers, touching her heart. "I'm here, baby. Watch me while I love you."

She cried out. "Yes! Please."

She gasped as he lapped, and her body burned and shook for release. His tongue circled her pleasure point, and a powerful climax gripped her full-force as she shuddered.

Ridge groaned and shifted himself up. He pressed the head of his erection inside her. Claire moaned at the luxury of his size.

He whispered a curse, brushing messy strands of

hair off her face. "Claire, you're perfect. And you're mine." His hips moved forward. He inched in deeper. "Is this too much at once? Are you okay?"

She sighed. "I'm more than okay. You just made sure of that with your mouth." She kissed him. "It's been a while. But you were worth the wait, my sweet man."

"You're worth double the wait," he whispered, gliding deeper, and her body quivered. "Claire. You're special. *We're* special." He dropped a kiss onto her lips. "I want that, you know? *Us*. As a couple. Do you want it too?"

"More than I can say," she whispered, clasping his face. "Ridge, I don't know how long I can last." His enthusiasm had primed her body for another quick release. "You're big, and I want you so much."

He thrusted his hips, and her heat pulsed. She accepted him deeper.

Within minutes, she hurtled toward the brink again.

"Give into it," he whispered against her mouth. "Claire. Be here with me. Now. I'm two seconds from losing control." He kneaded her breasts. "Make that one second."

He swiveled his pelvis, and her heart folded in

on itself, her world blazing with sparkling light. He stole her breath as his climax rippled, joining hers.

As she soared over the edge and into a lifetime with her man, Claire fell in love.

Epilogue

Seven months later
Tuesday morning, February 13th

R‍IDGE SORTED clothes in the laundry hamper he shared with Claire. Dressed in a clean pair of personal scrubs in front of the appliance closet, he stuffed her clothes into the washer and saved his gear for the next load. When he'd moved in at the beginning of January, rearranging furniture to accommodate his desk and claiming drawers and hangars, Claire had said to call her place *their* place. But he still caught himself thinking of the spacious apartment as hers. He wasn't being a caveman.

Sometimes he woke up believing his life was a dream since meeting her last summer and falling in love. Claire was his gorgeous girlfriend and his sultry soulmate. If she accepted his proposal, she would become his fiancée...and then his treasured wife.

He patted his scrubs pants pocket, sending a glance down the hall toward the open bedroom door. Claire hadn't yet woken from a cozy slumber following their early morning lovemaking and a rose-scented bubble bath. She'd booked today and tomorrow away from the office to help synchronize their schedules. Her employer was great that way. After bringing her good friend Lacey's business into the Clemmons Consulting fold, Claire had accepted a promotion that included increased responsibility but greater flexibility, which worked perfectly for them as a couple.

Tomorrow was Valentine's Day, but Ridge wanted to surprise the hell out of his woman and pop the question a day early. He smiled. His nights as an event dancer might be behind him, but his stage was set. Nothing too fancy to rouse her suspicions. Over the last seven months, he'd learned she preferred heartfelt.

He started the washer, then made a show of

loudly singing about kissing a nightstick while closing and opening the laundry-closet doors. Belting out Claire's lyrics—forever committed to memory—he stomped into the kitchen. He pressed the coffeemaker button and called his dad. Voice booming, he asked about Ruth and Fargone.

Claire's footfalls padded as she came down the hall. Heart racing and palms chilly with nerves, Ridge disconnected and set aside his phone. He drank in the sight of his messy-haired love, sexy as a goddess in his red plaid robe. She crossed her arms and shot him a cute, chastising glare. His chest heated.

"Wow, I love you." The words tumbled from his mouth.

Sunshine burst across her face. "And I love you. To bits. But the deal was if I let you wake me at the butt-crack of dawn to satisfy your needs," she said sweetly, "you'd let me sleep in." She tapped a foot. "I don't smell the breakfast you promised either, although the coffee is a welcome start." She sniffed, inhaling brewing dark roast. "Mmm."

Ridge had satisfied *her* needs twice, but he wouldn't nit-pick.

"Aw, honey, you know I can't stand not to have you by my side." So true. Outside of their jobs and the rigors of medical school, they spent most of their days and nights together.

"And you know how grouchy I can get," she said.

When she didn't manage a full night's sleep. "Yep. I do."

Over the last nearly-six-but-who-was-counting weeks, they'd laughed, made love in every corner of the apartment, quarreled about his damp towels left on the bathroom floor and her bras showing up tangled in his sock drawer, and learned not to collide in the kitchen. Last August, Ridge met her family, and Claire got to know his dad and Ruth as soon as the pair returned from honeymoon. They'd video-chatted with his mom at Christmas. They fit into each other's friend groups, another sign they were meant to be.

"I also know how quick you are to take me back after we fight," he teased. Usually, their cuddle-fights led to meaningful lovemaking.

Her pale green eyes sparkled. "Take you back? Ridge, I haven't let you go since the night we met." She twirled a hand around the kitchen, and the robe sleeve sagged on her arm. "As long as you don't stock feeder mice in the fridge, you're my guy for life." She shrugged. "Well, you're my guy anyway."

"That's a relief." He dropped a kiss onto her

dewy lips. "Because I love living with you, Claire. I love *you*."

"Oh, Ridge. I love you. But you understand this is your place too?"

Yeah, they'd had this conversation a few times. "If this were my place, you might find a one-eyed snake slithering around." He pulled her close.

She giggled, curling her arms around his waist. "*Your* one-eyed snake is always welcome in my hiding cave."

His body responded to her nearness and their favorite inside joke.

"Seriously," she said with an appreciative glance down at his puffed-up scrubs. "If we ever need to snake-sit, can we do it at your dad and Ruth's place?"

Ridge nodded. "It beats carting Fargone's stuff here."

"Good." Hands on either side of his face, Claire kissed him. "Hearing you say you love me is the greatest thrill of my life. Every time."

"You're easy to please, but you deserve more." Ridge slid a hand into a scrubs pocket and got down on one knee. "Claire," he said, clasping her hand as he produced a simple engagement ring.

Her eyes grew wide. "Is that what I think it is?"

He squeezed her hand, holding the delicate ring between his left thumb and forefinger. "If you think this is an engagement ring and that I'm about to propose, you're right." He'd imagined the words coming out a lot smoother, but the prospect of getting engaged to this incredible woman had wiped his prepared speech from his brain.

Her free hand clapped over her heart. "Omigosh." She squeaked. Then shook her head. "Ridge, I love the ring, and I adore you. Truly." She drew in a shaky breath. "We agreed you wouldn't spend money you need for school on a ring. I can't believe I'm saying this,"—she swallowed—"but can you take it back?"

Ridge chuckled. "Claire." He stood and grazed a thumb on her cheek. "This was my great-grandmother's ring on my dad's side. I know it's not elaborate. Someday I'll buy you a two-carat replacement ring."

She gasped. "*What*? No, you won't. I want this one." She grabbed the ring out of his hand. "Sorry," she said, blinking at the diamond. "We should start over."

He laughed. "We should."

She tucked the ring into his palm, her fingers warm on his knuckles. "First, you need to know that when you ask me to marry you, I'm wearing *this* ring until the band thins to a thread. Bear in mind, that might take sixty years."

Ridge nodded, emotion swelling in his throat. He lowered and presented the ring in both hands. "Claire Merriweather, before I met you, I'd heard about this thing called love at first sight, but didn't think it would ever happen to me. After what my mom and dad went through, I literally thought I'd be the last guy to meet his wife at a bachelorette party and later again in a basement laundry room. Wearing practically nothing. But that's what happened with you and me. You caught me by surprise, Claire Merriweather, and I love you deeply for it."

She beamed a smile of pure happiness. "You caught me by surprise too," she whispered. "*And* in your arms, as I recall. You continue to surprise me."

"Do you like surprises?"

She nodded. "Especially when they include you."

"Then will you make me the happiest man and be my wife?"

"Yes! Yes, yes!"

He slipped the ring onto her finger. "One more thing," he said, reaching for his phone and selecting a curated play list from his stripping days.

"Ridge, the ring is perfect," Claire murmured, voice dreamy, as if she hadn't heard him.

A cover of a 1970s disco tune streamed from the phone, the singer crooning about a last chance and romance. Ridge rocked his hips, and he and Claire kissed and hugged as she smiled and swayed in his arms. The robe trailed on the floor.

"Should I take this as a sign that you're sexy-dancing for me tonight?" She asked him with a flirty look.

Ridge kissed his fiancée, his heart overflowing with hopes and dreams for their future. And with enduring love. "For the rest of our lives, honey, *all* my dances are for you."

Don't miss *Before Brady*, the next book in the series! *Before Brady* features Alicia Maxwell, one of the bridesmaids in the upcoming wedding (if it happens), and sexy cop, Brady Jacobs.

Get your copy of *Before Brady*!

The story

Alicia Maxwell feels pulled in a million directions, trying to make her cupcake shop a success. Nothing will stand in her way. Especially not sexy cop Brady Jacobs, who gave her a speeding ticket with a twinkle in his eyes. Then claimed he was just doing his job!

But when chaos erupts in the weeks before a friend's wedding, Brady turns on the help. And the charm. Ultra-focused Alicia needs neither. Not his fiery touches. Or his sweet kisses. Not—

Oh, no, *what* is happening? Before long, Alicia yearns for Brady's heart and his arms...but has she missed her chance?

Before Brady Preview
Steamy RomCom
by Cindy Procter-King

Saturday night, July 15th

Countdown to Tania and Trey's wedding: 14 days

(unless...)

"Ready?" Alicia Maxwell asked her assistant, Lettie. They stood in the reception hall kitchen, wearing matching gold T-shirts and mint-green miniskirts. On the other side of the swinging door, three hundred thirtieth anniversary party guests laughed and clapped as the host delivered a heartfelt toast to his wife.

Lettie's brown eyes widened. "Y-yes." The hesitation in the younger woman's voice suggested otherwise.

Alicia touched her assistant's arm. "Promise

you're not just saying that? Because I can do it." Although she didn't want to, if it could be helped. Alicia didn't want Brady Jacobs to catch sight of her at all during his parents' celebration. Which meant staying in the catering kitchen while Lettie carried in the slicing cake for three large cupcake towers sitting on the dessert table.

Lettie drew in a ragged breath. "I'll make last night up to you if it's the last thing I do."

Alicia smiled. "I wouldn't want it to be the *last* thing you do. Please don't worry about the first batch of cupcakes. I need you, Lettie. We're a team."

Lettie shook her head. Her springy curls bounced. "You're my boss. And I'm a nitwit."

"That's not true." Given the twenty-two-year-old's baking experience and delicious sample cupcakes, Lettie required more supervision than Alicia had expected. Nothing more. "We're both bagged." Flat-out exhausted.

Lettie's lower lip trembled. "Because of me."

"No. Because of *my* choices." Alicia inhaled, her frustration directed at herself. In her quest to grow Bitty Cakes as quickly as possible, she'd accepted too many catering jobs this summer. Squeezing in the Jacobs anniversary had increased a heavy workload. The stress was doing a number on herself as well as her employees. If Alicia were into assigning blame, *she* was the nitwit.

Last night, she'd jumped at Lettie's offer to bake three hundred cupcakes on her own. In hindsight, not a smart move, but Alicia understood Lettie's need to prove herself. As the baby of the Maxwell family and the only girl out of five kids, Alicia had struggled not to feel singled out, while also somehow getting lost in the mix, since the early death of her mom.

Before abandoning Lettie yesterday to handle the humongous anniversary order, Alicia had described tweaks to the shop's popular mint chocolate chip recipe. Unfortunately, she'd neglected to highlight an important ingredient adjustment.

Um, yeah. Not so bright.

Believing everything under control, Alicia hurried home to host a friend's combination bridal shower and bachelorette party. Lettie was to text or call with questions. Alicia hadn't heard a word.

She *should* have followed up with her assistant. If the shower hadn't escalated into a rowdy extravaganza, she would have checked in with Lettie earlier.

As it was, the muscular stripper whipped the women into a frenzy. The winner of the scavenger hunt became enamored with another guest's brother. The bride took 'tipsy' to a new level, which remained a bit of a mystery because Alicia hadn't noticed Tania tossing them back.

As the festivities wound down, Alicia walked the bride to a nearby park before driving her home. Everything had felt relatively manageable to that point.

Way too long later, she'd spotted her phone dead in her purse. Upon plugging in, several panicked texts and voicemails flooded her screen. Each from an overwhelmed Lettie, requesting Alicia's help and guidance.

Alicia had needed to redo three...hundred... cupcakes...while her assistant slept off a well-deserved rest.

She stifled a yawn. "Let's put last night behind us," she urged Lettie. "How about we channel serenity?" She swept up her hands in a reassuring gesture. "We're calm. We're collected. We take charge of our actions and our lives."

Lettie repeated the motions. "We're calm. We're collected. *Phew*. Thank you, Alicia."

"You're welcome." Alicia stepped to the kitchen's swinging door and cracked it open. She peered inside the hall.

Twenty feet away, Brady's mom joined his dad at the decorated podium. The couple addressed the crowd, and a spike of unease skittered up Alicia's spine. A natural response, she told herself. At this early phase of her business, coordinating desserts for large occasions required every ounce of her focus. Tonight was no different.

Except...except...tonight *was* different, damn it. Alicia chewed her lip. Although she hadn't spotted him, knowing Brady Jacobs sat at a family table sent pinpricks of sensation along her limbs and across her face.

She couldn't allow anything else to go wrong at *his* parents' shindig. She hadn't fully recovered from their last encounter. Obsessing over his unsettling effect on her nervous system took a toll she lacked the time or energy to process.

She focused her attention onto his mom, Maureen. One word from the woman would signal the delivery of the slicing cake.

"Dessert!" Maureen announced, and cheers filled the enormous room.

Alicia glanced around the hall. The family and friends in attendance spanned generations from a crying baby to a ninety-year-old man. Children played between the crowded tables. Teenagers huddled along a wall. An exasperated-looking woman raced after a toddler clutching a cupcake. The adorable monster squealed with glee each time he evaded the harried woman's grasp.

Despite the commotion, Don and Maureen Jacobs exchanged loving smiles. The couple planned to feed each other bites of cake, like a bride and groom. Alicia sighed. They were so sweet.

She looked back at Lettie, who picked up the six-inch slicing cake on a sturdy tray.

"Piece o' cake," Lettie said with a grin.

"That's the spirit." Alicia opened the kitchen door, and Lettie walked out.

A boisterous, "Hurrah!" boomed from the crowd.

Alicia peeked into the hall again, monitoring Lettie's progress toward the dessert table, situated to the left of Brady's parents. After accounting for the cupcake theft, two-hundred-ninety-nine tasty desserts adorned the display towers. The edible gold stars Brady's mom had requested decorated the mint-green frosting spirals. The spangles reminded Alicia of Brady's police badge. Although his star was silver. And bigger. A *lot* bigger.

Oh, for—

She shook her head. The size of Brady's badge wasn't relevant. Tonight's cupcakes looked and tasted divine. She had consumed several lopsided extras to make sure.

Her gaze found him—although she hadn't been looking for the guy. He sat at a round table near the podium, a frown creasing his handsome face. Alicia took in his short-trimmed chestnut-brown hair with a hint of curl at the crown. Her heart did an annoying leap-for-joy thing. *Down, girl.*

She allowed herself a scan of his broad chest in a white dress shirt before hauling her gaze back up to his expression. Her eyebrows arched. Why was he frowning? Was he surprised *she* wasn't bringing in the slicing cake? Was he wondering why she hadn't shown her face tonight?

Not that it mattered, but let him stew over—uh, consider the ramifications of issuing her a speeding ticket three weeks ago. Yeah, let him.

The moment she'd recognized him at her car window, she'd insisted he not treat her differently from any other driver, even if she was his comman-der's daughter. It was embarrassing enough that she hadn't realized she was traveling well over the posted limit, so intent had she been on locating the supply store his mom had specified for purchasing the edible stars.

True, Alicia had made a valuable new contact in

the bakery industry, but the fact remained that *Officer* Brady Jacobs had caught her with her pedal to the infernal metal. In her family, traffic infractions were grounds for lecturing to the extreme.

"Just doing my job," Brady had said that fateful Saturday. He'd tipped his police hat, his mesmerizing green eyes twinkling.

The memory swirled, and Alicia's body warmed.

As he'd returned to his patrol unit, she'd eyed his butt in her side mirror. Again, only later had she noticed a lower speed recorded on her ticket, saving her a hefty fine and eliminating a hike in her insurance rates.

Brady had orchestrated the favor behind her back! The man had some nerve.

Squaring her shoulders, Alicia scoped out Lettie's snail-like progress toward the dessert table. Maureen smiled and stepped closer to the girl.

Brady sprang off his chair.

Alicia followed his gaze to a glob of frosting on the floor.

In Lettie's path.

"Oh, no," she whispered, extending a hand, heart ticking like a doomsday countdown. "L-Lettie," she said louder. "Watch your step."

Lettie skidded on the frosting and crashed to her backside.

The cake catapulted into the air.

A collective gasp burst from the crowd.

Alicia dashed into the hall. *"Oh, my God,"* she muttered hoarsely. "This cannot be happening."

But it was.

Brady's mom leaped toward the cake. Maureen's arms scooped forward as if she were trying to catch a football. Or a bridal bouquet.

"Look out," Don shouted.

A young woman rushed over. "Mom. No!"

Brady tried holding back his mom, but Maureen flung off his arm.

The cake hit Maureen's ivory lace dress. Mint-green frosting smashed into her cleavage. Chunks of cake spewed into the air and onto the ground. The tray clattered to the floor.

Maureen swiped at her bodice. "Our cake! Don, I thought I had it in my sights."

Alicia reached the family. "Maureen! I'm so sorry."

"We're good," Don responded, not unkindly. He nodded toward Lettie, who wept on the ground, cradling her head. "See to your assistant."

"Of course." Alicia kneeled beside her employee. "Here, Lettie. Take my hand."

Lettie groaned, sobs wracking her shoulders.

Alicia alternated between scanning her assistant for injuries and gawking as Brady grabbed two fistfuls of paper napkins and passed them to his father.

The young woman who'd hurried to Maureen retrieved the tray and disappeared from view. Don wiped his wife's dress as dozens of friends and family gathered close.

A man hoisted a champagne glass. "As Jacobs parties go, this one takes the cupcake!"

The crowd laughed.

Maureen flicked a hand. "I'm all right. It's only cake."

Don dipped a finger into her cleavage and made a show of licking off the frosting. "Tastes great," he declared, digging in for seconds.

The crowd hooted and cheered.

"Don," Maureen cooed. She smiled at Alicia. "Don't worry, honey. Tend to your friend."

Alicia *would* worry. Maureen's dress was a mess, and hundreds of guests had witnessed a cupcake disaster of epic proportions. Phone cameras abounded. Bitty Cakes would become a laughing-stock. And poor Lettie—

Brady lowered beside Alicia and her employee. "Stay back, everyone," he said, holding up a hand. His gaze flicked to Lettie's. "Don't move."

Alicia waved him away. "I have First Aid."

"I can handle this."

"So can I." She stared into his dazzling moss-green eyes. She refused to allow them to hypnotize her into compliance. Lettie was her responsibility.

Lettie wailed. "I'm a failure!"

Alicia examined her assistant's head and body. "Lettie, shh. Where does it hurt?"

Lettie sniffled. "I didn't hit my head. I thought I did, but my butt is sore."

Brady nodded. "I'll take you to the hospital."

Alicia lifted her chin. "I'll take her."

His gaze swept over the crowded room. "You have your hands full," he pointed out.

"Right." With Lettie out of commission, Alicia represented the sole member of the dessert catering staff. Thankfully, a second slicing cake sat in the kitchen. Call her paranoid, but after her mistake with the recipe, she'd considered it prudent to bake a spare.

A dark-skinned guy around Lettie's age crouched beside them. "I'm more than happy to drive Lettie to the hospital. We've met before.

Haven't we, Lets?" The fellow patted Lettie's arm.

Lettie's eyes opened from between splayed fingers. "Y-yes." She gave the dude a watery smile. "Thank you."

Brady nodded at the younger man. "Way to step up, Nelson." He glanced at Alicia. "Our parents live on the same road. I've known Nelson since he was in diapers."

"TMI," Nelson quipped, helping Lettie.

The younger woman winced as she stood. "I'm sorry, Alicia. I shouldn't have taken this job. I don't have the experience."

Alicia popped to her feet. "That's okay. Um, what do you mean?"

"My mom—" Lettie sucked in a breath. "My mom baked my sample cupcakes."

"What?" Alicia's pulse blipped. During Lettie's five months of employment, Alicia had supervised the girl through countless recipes. "I checked your references. The bakery in Auburn gave a glowing review."

"That was a friend. Working at a cupcake shop sounded fun. My friend said I would learn. But this job is stressful. I can't take it anymore. I quit."

Alicia's jaw hit the floor. Lettie had chosen *now*

to come clean? In front of hundreds of potential customers?

Brady leaned close. "Let's go to the kitchen," he murmured. "I'll help."

"I can manage on my own," Alicia muttered, cursing the ticklish sensation rippling up her neck.

His mom stepped forward. "Alicia, please accept my apologies. I pressured you into taking this job on short notice. Brady said his fellow officers gobble your cupcakes every chance they get. And your father—well, Brady says the man just raves."

Alicia's cheeks burned. She didn't want to hear about Brady's connection to her dad. She loved her family, but she'd worked hard to achieve her independence.

"I will take care of everything tonight," she reiterated with a stiff smile. She glimpsed Nelson and Lettie exiting the building. She returned her attention to Brady's mom. "Maureen, I'll pay for your dry cleaning and discount the catering bill." She backed toward the kitchen. "I'll get the spare slicing cake—"

"Don't worry your sweet head about it." Maureen paused. "Oh. Did you say you have a spare?"

Alicia nodded. Her one saving grace today. She had a spare.

"I'll be back soon," she said, arrowing for the kitchen. Oh, boy, she would never hear the end about tonight. Once her dad and her four older brothers caught wind of this latest upheaval, they would fall all over her with advice and good intentions instead of allowing her to stand—or fail, if it came to that—on her own.

"Alicia, wait." Brady's deep voice resonated with concern and earthy sexiness.

But she dared not glance back. She dared not allow the man to slip beneath her defenses for one enticing moment. He touched an emotion deep inside her which could swallow her up in romantic fantasies.

She couldn't allow that. *Could not.* She needed to stay on point. In her life and in her business.

He needed to find another woman to rescue.

Find out more at:

www.cindyprocter-king.com

Acknowledgments

Thank you to my friend Jamie Kain for help researching the "snake bits." Any errors or embellishments are mine.

Also, thanks to Mary J. Forbes for reading and critiquing an earlier version of this story. Your input is always invaluable.

My husband rode a motorcycle for 19 years, so I didn't have to research how to carefully dismount from the passenger seat. It's drilled into my brain!

As for how to ride as a passenger, "just float."

You're welcome. :)

Cindy

About the Author

Cindy Procter-King writes steamy romcoms and contemporary romances bursting with laughter and emotion. Sassy feel-good fiction!

Cindy's books are available from eBook retailers all over the world, as well as in trade paperback, some library hardcover and large print, and some foreign editions.

Cindy lives in Canada with her family, Ghost'Da Allie McBeagle, and too many grand-dogs to count!

For more books and updates, visit:
www.cindyprocter-king.com

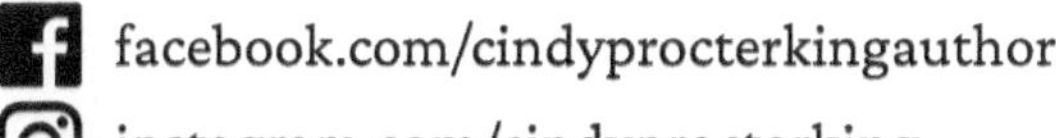

facebook.com/cindyprocterkingauthor

instagram.com/cindyprocterking

bookbub.com/authors/cindy-procter-king

twitter.com/cindypk

Crave another sassy romance?

www.readsassyromance.com

www.ingramcontent.com/pod-product-compliance
Lightning Source LLC
Chambersburg PA
CBHW031057310726
48969CB00007B/2319